ME AND MY AFRO

BY Aiden M. Taylor

ILLUSTRATED BY TANA TEEYA

250 East 54th Street, Suite P2
New York, New York 10022

www.lightswitchlearning.com

Educators and Librarians, for a variety of teaching resources, visit www.lightswitchlearning.com.

Cover design and illustrations by Tana Teeya

ISBN: 978-1-7354085-1-4

Printed in China

This book belongs to: _____

Hi, my name is Aiden, and I have a really BIG Afro.

We go to school together.

7

We go to the library together.

8

We go to the store together.

We go to the park together.

We go to the beach together.

We play basketball together.

We go to birthday parties together.

15

We go to the movie theater together.

We go to the museum together.

19

Sometimes, my Afro is so small.

I love it all!

21

And I love ME!

23

About The Author

Photo by Tim Taylor

Aiden M. Taylor is a ten-year-old boy who has been viewed by millions in television commercials and Times Square billboards. But now he wants to be more than just seen; Aiden has a big message for children in his new book, *Me and My Afro*. "I want kids to love and be themselves," he says.

If quarantine is good enough for Shakespeare (who likely wrote *King Lear* during the plague isolation), it's good enough for Aiden. He came up with the idea for his empowering picture book during the COVID-19 lockdown after contemplating the opinions that so many people have about his substantial hair.

When friends would tell him he needed a haircut, Aiden would consider this suggestion with his mom, who was sure to let him know that his hair always looks good. "Our hair is such a big part of our identity," says Aiden, "[so] I felt it was a good message to get out there."

This fifth-grader has big dreams with his debut book, *Me and My Afro*: "to show other kids the importance of loving yourself and embracing your hair and that all kids were created special."

When Aiden is not writing books, he works as an actor and model and loves basketball, video games, poetry, math, and researching and learning new things. He is a "Proud Little Brother," a part of the Big Brothers Big Sisters of New York City program.

And, by the way, Aiden also thinks he—and his hair—look super cool as a picture book illustration.